W9-COH-021

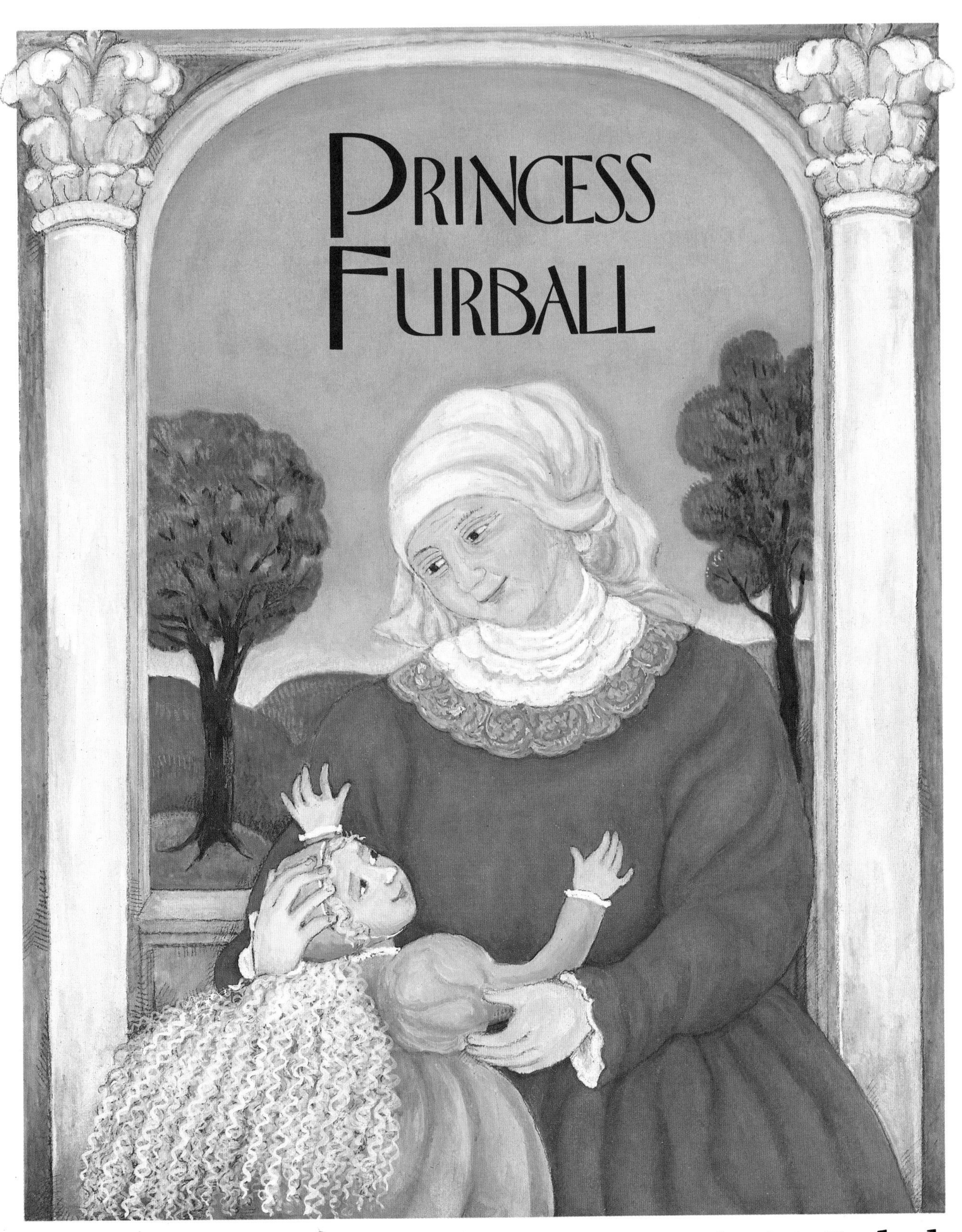

Retold by **Charlotte Huck** · Illustrated by **Anita Lobel**

GREENWILLOW BOOKS NEW YORK

"Furball," one of the many variants of the Cinderella story, was my favorite childhood fairy tale. Readers will recognize it as being similar to the English "Catskin," and to the Grimms' "Many Furs" or "Thousand Furs." With the exception of the well-known French Cinderella tale with its glass slipper ending, this variant with the "hated marriage" motif is the most popular of the more than five hundred variants of the Cinderella story. Many of these tales included an unlawful marriage or incestuous theme. In rewriting this version, I believe I have been faithful to the psychological truth of the earlier tellings.

Charlotte Huck

Redlands, California

Watercolor and gouache paints were used for the full-color art.
The text type is ITC Berkeley.

Printed in Singapore by Tien Wah Press
First Edition 10 9 8 7 6 5 4 3 2 1

Library of Congress Cataloging-in-Publication Data

Huck, Charlotte Princess Furball
by Charlotte Huck; pictures by Anita Lobel p. cm.
Summary: A princess in a coat of a thousand furs hides her identity from a king who falls in love with her.
ISBN 0-688-07837-0. ISBN 0-688-07838-9 (lib. bdg.)
[1. Fairy tales. 2. Folklore—England.]
I. Lobel, Anita, ill. II. Title. PZ8.H862Fu 1989
398.2'0942—dc19 [E] 88-18780 CIP AC

In memory of Ginny, who loved this tale as much as her twin sister does

Once upon a time there was a beautiful young Princess whose hair was the color of pure gold. She was frequently lonely and unhappy, for her mother had died when she was a baby, and her father paid little attention to her.

Luckily, her old nurse, who loved the Princess as a mother loves a daughter, saw that she was lonely and allowed her to run and play with the village children. And some days the Princess visited with the Cook in the large kitchen and learned to make soup and bread and cakes. Yet the nurse never forgot that the young girl was a princess. She taught her the manners of a lady and arranged for tutors to instruct her in reading, writing, and dancing. And so the Princess grew to be strong and capable and clever, besides being beautiful.

One day the old nurse died, and the Princess felt all alone again. To make matters worse, her father promised her hand in marriage to an Ogre who agreed to give the King fifty wagons of silver in return.

The Princess was horrified when she heard what her father had done, and begged him to change his mind. But her father was determined to carry out his bargain. The Princess then thought of a clever plan. "Father," she said, "before I marry I must have three bridal gifts—one dress as golden as the sun, another as silvery as the moon, and a third as glittering as the stars. In addition, I shall need a coat made of a thousand different kinds of fur, one piece from every animal in your kingdom."

"There," she thought, "my father will never be able to meet these demands."

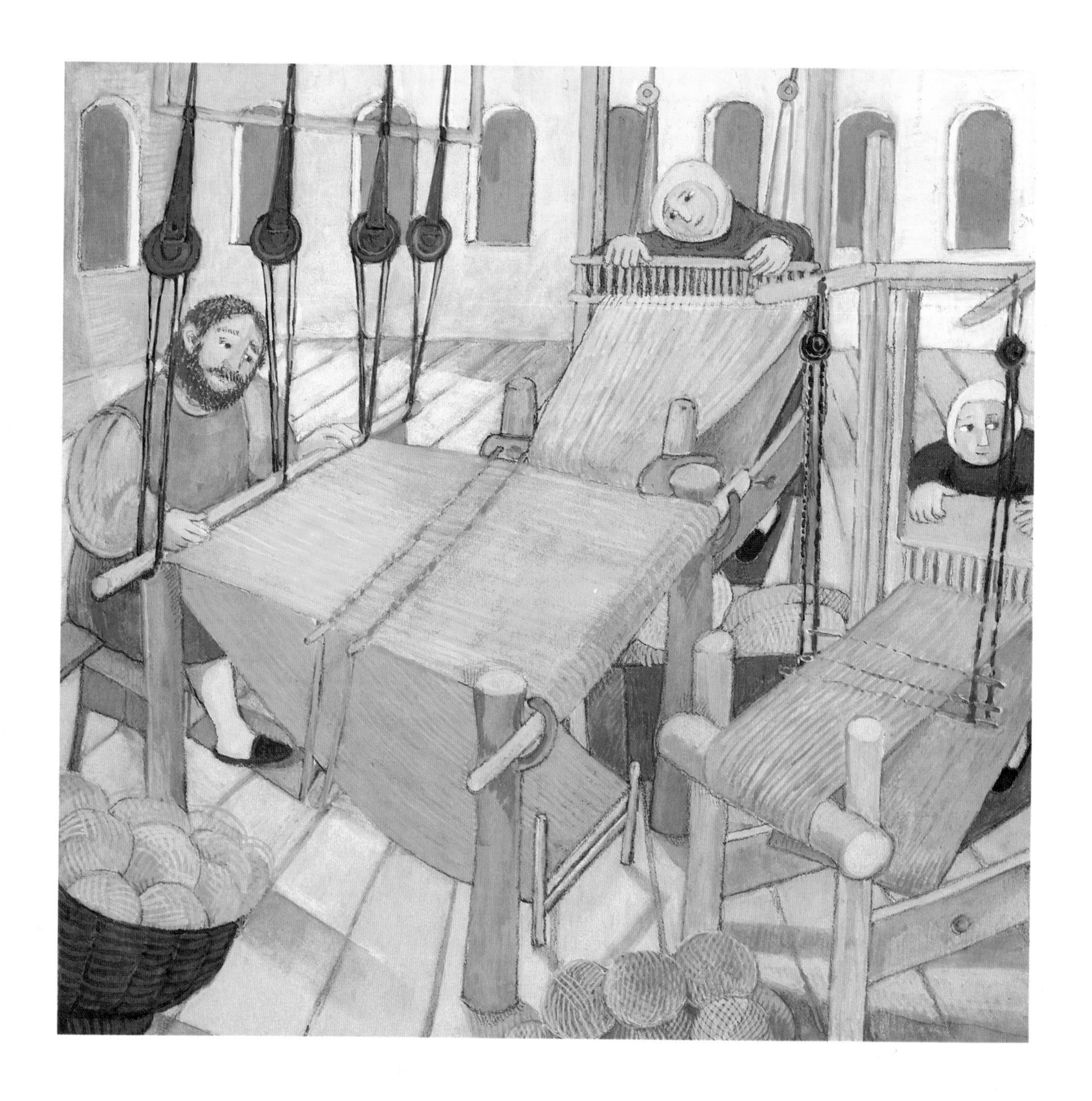

The King, however, began at once to provide for her bridal gifts. He called for the most skillful weavers in the land and ordered them to weave three dresses—one as golden as the sun, another as silvery as the moon, and the third as glittering as the stars.

He commanded his hunters to go into the forest, kill a thousand different kinds of wild animals, and bring home their skins so that the coat could be made. At last, when all the gifts were ready, the King laid them out for his daughter to see and said, "Tomorrow your marriage will take place."

The poor Princess decided the only thing to do was run away.

That night, when all the castle was asleep, the Princess got up. She folded the sun, the moon, and the star dresses into a package so small that it could fit in a walnut shell. Then she took three tiny treasures that had belonged to her mother: a gold ring, a gold thimble, and a little gold spinning wheel. These she put into a second walnut shell. Into a third shell she put her favorite seasoning for the soup the Cook had taught her to make. Then she bound up her hair, put on her boots and her coat of a thousand furs, and stepped out into the silent snowy darkness. She walked all night.

At dawn the Princess came to a thick forest. She was very tired. The snow had covered her footprints, so she knew she could safely stop and rest. She found a hollow tree, curled up in it, and fell asleep. The sun rose higher and higher, but the Princess slept on until it was nearly noon.

On this very day, the young King to whom the woods belonged was out hunting in the forest. His hounds came to the tree where the Princess slept, and they began to sniff and run around and around, barking excitedly. The King called to his hunters and said, "Go see what is hiding in that tree."

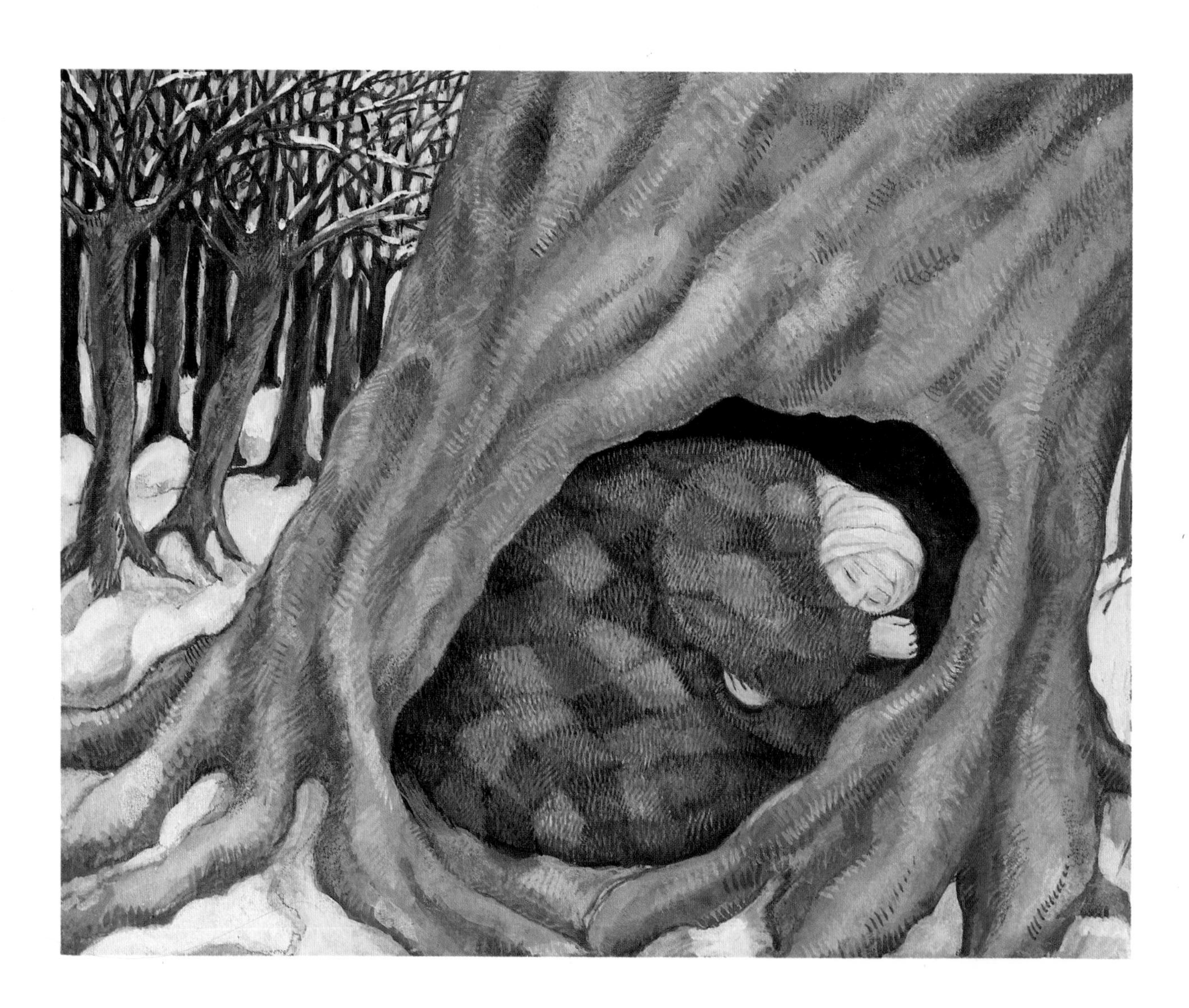

Two hunters went over to look. When they came back, they told the King that they had found a marvelous creature sound asleep in the hollow of the tree. "Its body is covered with a thousand different kinds of fur," they said.

"See if you can capture it alive," said the King. "Then tie it up, put it into the wagon, and bring it back to the castle."

When the hunters grabbed the Princess, she woke up in terror and cried out, "Please don't hurt me. I have no home. Have pity on me and take me with you."

"Well," they said. "Come along, little Furball, we'll take you to the Cook. Perhaps he can find something useful for you to do. You can at least sweep up the ashes for him."

The hunters put Furball into the wagon and drove her to the King's castle. There they showed her an old woodshed where daylight never entered. "Furball, you may live and sleep here," they said. Then they took her to the kitchen, where the Cook had her fetch the wood, draw the water, stir the fire, pluck the chickens, clean the vegetables, wash the dishes, sweep the ashes, and do all the rest of the dirty work that no one else wanted to do.

Poor Furball lived for a long time as a servant to the servants. She could not see how her life would ever change.

One day Furball heard that the King was giving a ball at the castle. "Please," she said to the Cook, "may I go for a little while to see the guests arrive? I promise you that no one will catch even a glimpse of me."

"Go," said the gruff old Cook, "but be back in half an hour to sweep up the ashes and put the kitchen in order."

Furball quickly took her smoky oil lamp and darted to her little woodshed. She washed the soot and ashes from her face and hands and undid her hair. Then she opened the first walnut shell and took out the dress that was as golden as the sun. Its glow lit up the whole woodshed.

As soon as the Princess was ready, she slipped around to the front of the castle and entered the great door as a guest. No one recognized her as Furball, the cinder maid of the kitchen. The doorkeepers thought she was a princess from some other country, and they bowed to her as she entered. They quickly told the King of her arrival, and he hastened to greet the Princess and lead her out to dance.

"Never have I seen anyone so beautiful and charming," he thought to himself as they danced.

When the music stopped, the Sun Princess curtsied to the King and smiled at him so brightly that his eyes were dazzled. Before he knew what had happened, she seemed to vanish. The guard at the castle gate was called and questioned, but he had seen no one pass.

The Princess ran like a sunbeam to her dark shed. She took off her gleaming dress, put on her fur coat, smudged her face and hands with soot, and was once again Furball.

When she entered the kitchen and reached for the broom to sweep up the ashes, the Cook said, "Let that go until tomorrow. I want you to make some soup for the King so that I have a chance to see the visitors at the ball. But do not let one of your hairs drop into the soup, or you will get nothing to eat for a week."

While making the King's soup, Furball opened the nutshell that contained the special herbs and sprinkled some into the soup pot. When the soup was ready, she poured it into the King's bowl. Then she took her mother's gold ring from the other nutshell and quietly dropped it into the bowl.

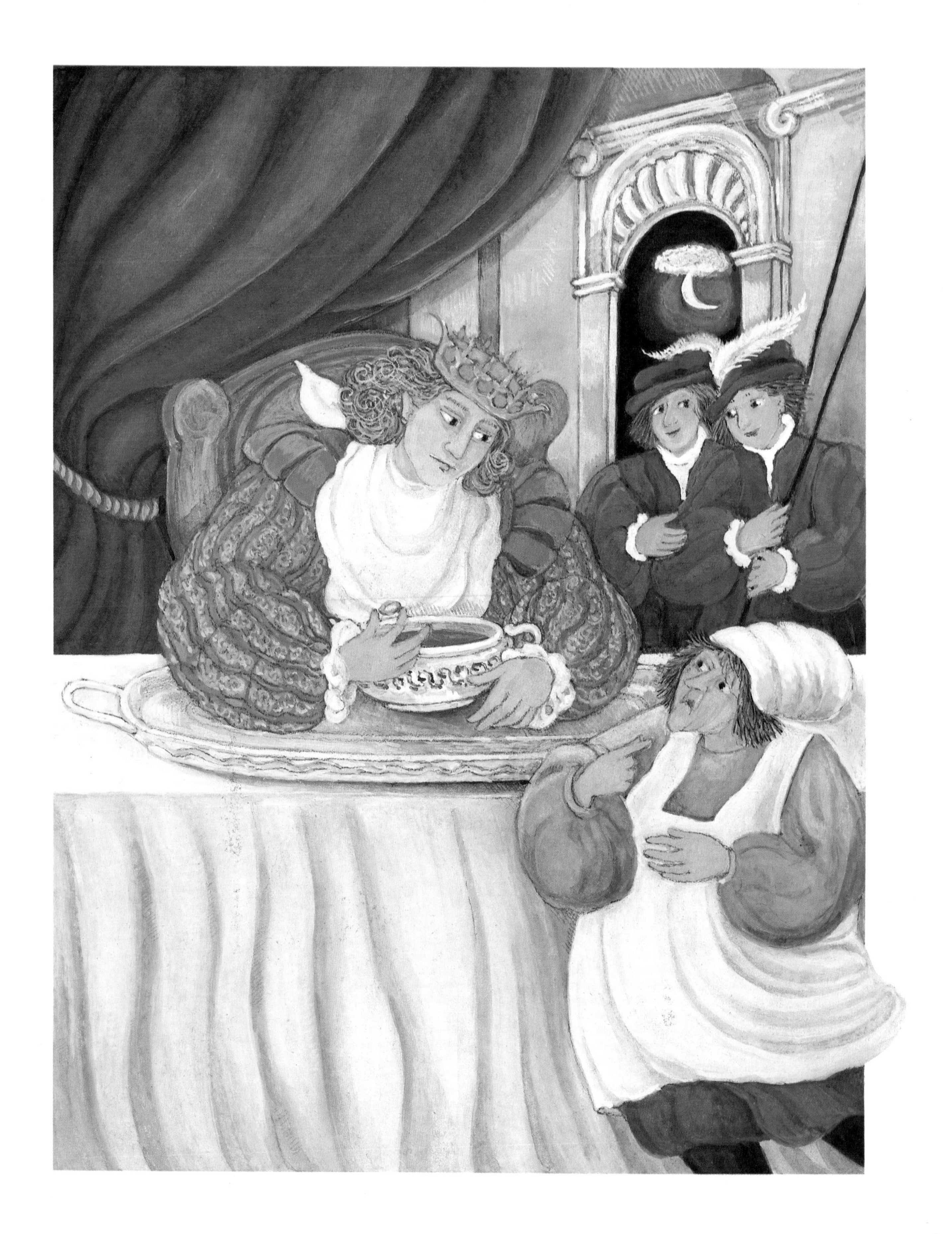

After the ball was over, the King called for his supper, and declared he had never tasted better soup in his life. But when the bowl was nearly empty, he discovered to his surprise the small gold ring at the bottom. He could not imagine how it got there and ordered the Cook to appear before him.

The old Cook was terribly frightened. "You must have let a hair fall into the soup," he growled at Furball. "If you have, I shall give you a good beating and nothing to eat for a week."

As soon as the Cook came into the banquet hall, the King demanded, "Who made this soup?"

"I–I made it, Sir," faltered the Cook.

"That is not true," said the King. "This soup is much better than any you have ever made."

Then the Cook had to confess that Furball had made the soup.

"Send her to me," commanded the King.

In no time at all Furball appeared, all covered with soot and stains. The King looked at her and said, "Who are you and how did you learn to make such good soup?"

"I am a stranger in your kingdom, Sir. I once worked in the kitchen of another castle where I learned to make soup."

"What do you know about this ring, which I found in my soup?" the King asked. But Furball only looked at him and would not answer.

When the King found he could learn nothing from her, he sent Furball away.

Sometime later there was another ball at the castle. Again Furball asked the Cook if she could go and watch the guests arrive.

"Go," he grunted, "but be sure to be back in one half hour to make the King that soup he is so fond of."

Furball promised to be back in one half hour and ran quickly to her little shed. There she washed off the stains and soot from her face and hands, and let down her hair. Then she took her dress as silvery as the moon out of the walnut shell and put it on. Again the shed shone with the light of her dress.

She appeared at the castle door as a foreign princess, just as she had done before. Only this time the King was waiting for her. He was so glad to see her that he would dance with no one else. But at the end of the half hour, the Princess curtsied and vanished as quickly as she had before.

Like a moonbeam she slipped around the castle and back down to her little shed where she made herself once again into the sooty little Furball. Then she returned to the kitchen to make the King's soup.

This time, after adding the special herbs, Furball dropped the tiny gold thimble into the King's bowl.

The King ate the soup with great relish, but was amazed to find the gold thimble at the bottom of the bowl.

Again he sent for the Cook and asked him if he had made the soup. And again the Cook confessed that it was Furball. She was ordered to appear before the King, but when he asked her about the gold thimble, she only looked at him and would not say a word.

At the King's third ball everything happened as before. The Cook told Furball that she might go and see the guests arrive. "But be sure you are back in time to make that soup the King thinks is better than mine," he growled.

Furball did not stop to listen, but ran quickly to her shed, washed off her stains and soot, combed her golden hair, and put on the dress that glittered like the stars.

When the King stepped forward to receive her in the hall, as he had done twice before, he thought her quite the most beautiful maiden in the world. He knew that he had fallen in love with her. While they were dancing he slipped the tiny gold ring onto her finger.

The King had asked the musicians to play the longest dance they knew, but the minute the music stopped, the Princess smiled at him and was gone like a shooting star.

The Princess was out of breath when she reached the shed and knew she had overstayed her time. She quickly tied a scarf around her hair, threw her fur coat over her star dress, and began to put soot and ashes on her face and hands. When she reached the kitchen she made the King's soup with its special seasoning, and then dropped the tiny gold spinning wheel into the bowl.

When he found the gold spinning wheel at the bottom of the bowl, the King sent for Furball. This time as she entered he looked at her hand, and there was the small gold ring, which she had not had the time to take off.

The King caught Furball by the hand, and while she struggled to get free the fur coat fell open and he saw the star dress. The King drew off Furball's coat of a thousand furs, and as he did so her scarf came off and her golden hair fell over her shoulders. Furball wiped the soot from her face and hands with her scarf, and stood before the King as the most radiant Princess on earth.

The King told the Princess he loved her and asked her to marry him. "You have the beauty of the sun, the moon, and the stars. You are as clever as you are lovely," he said, "and I cannot live without you."

Then the Princess told the King her story, and he loved her even more than before. The wedding took place the next day. Everyone who had attended the balls came to see the marriage of Furball and the King. The Cook, who made better pastries than soup, stayed up all night baking an enormous cake for the bridal couple.

And the King and his new Queen lived happily ever after.